*The Whirlpool*

# The Whirlpool

STORIES BY
## Laurel Croza

ILLUSTRATIONS BY
## Kelsey Garrity-Riley

GROUNDWOOD BOOKS
HOUSE OF ANANSI PRESS
TORONTO  BERKELEY

Groundwood Books / House of Anansi Press
groundwoodbooks.com

We acknowledge for their financial support of our publishing program
the Canada Council for the Arts, the Ontario Arts Council
and the Government of Canada.

Canada Council    Conseil des Arts
for the Arts      du Canada

ONTARIO ARTS COUNCIL
CONSEIL DES ARTS DE L'ONTARIO
an Ontario government agency
un organisme du gouvernement de l'Ontario

With the participation of the Government of Canada    | Canadä
Avec la participation du gouvernement du Canada

Library and Archives Canada Cataloguing in Publication
Croza, Laurel, author
The whirlpool : stories / Laurel Croza ; illustrated by Kelsey
Garrity-Riley.
Issued in print and electronic formats.
ISBN 978-1-77306-032-3 (hardcover).—ISBN 978-1-77306-033-0 (HTML).—
ISBN 978-1-77306-034-7 (Kindle)
I. Garrity-Riley, Kelsey, illustrator  II. Title.
PS8605.R698W45 2018          jC813'.6          C2017-905952-1
C2017-905953-X

Illustrations by Kelsey Garrity-Riley
Design by Michael Solomon

Groundwood Books is committed to protecting our natural environment. As part of our efforts, the interior of this book is printed on paper that contains 100% post-consumer recycled fibers, is acid-free and is processed chlorine-free.

Printed and bound in Canada

MIX
Paper from
responsible sources
FSC® C016245

In memory of Winnie Croza and Sheila Barry.
And for Mike, always. xo

# Contents

# It's a Step

When I was a little girl I loved playing Father, May I? at recess.

"Father, may I take seven small steps forward?"

"Four and a half bunny hops?"

"One giant leap?"

But I'm not little anymore. And I'm not playing a schoolyard game this morning.

Not with him.

His hand is already on the doorknob, twisting it, by the time I force myself to ask.

"Can I go to the Markham Fair on Saturday?" I speak fast, fingers crossed he'll hear me out before he leaves for work. "Everyone's going, Mel's mom's driving, both ways," I say, tumbling my words down the hall towards his back.

But before they can reach him, he slams the door shut, and I'm left alone, rattled like the windows, talking to myself. "I … I'd be home by nine."

I drop my shoulders down to where they were before I asked and I take a couple of steps backwards, retreating into the kitchen to finish making my lunch for school.

I remember why I used to love playing Father, May I? It didn't matter if I had to take a step back or miss a turn or, even, start again, because I knew — I knew for certain — that at some point in the game, Father would have to say, "Yes, you may!"

I know better now.

•

My father's been talking less and slamming more since Mom told him she'd been offered a job at the Tim's drive-thru by the highway.

He made himself perfectly clear.

"First, it's a nothing job. Second — how many times do I have to tell you? You. Don't. Need. To.

Work," he said. Quietly. Almost a whisper.

He never shouts.

He's been talking less and slamming more since Mom didn't back down, like she usually does, after he said, "Period. End of discussion."

Instead, she took a deep sink-or-swim breath and she said, "John, I'm taking that job."

For the first time I can remember, she didn't plead when she spoke his name.

She'd made up her mind.

Last week my teacher, Ms. Jung, told Mom and me that if I work on it, keep up my marks, I can get a scholarship. "Any university would be happy to have you."

I will work hard.

I want to go far.

Away from him.

"Mom, you'll come with me," I said. We'd stopped for a doughnut on the way home after teacher interviews.

"How?" she said.

"You can get a job. Save."

"Who'd hire me?" He'd told her so many times, she believed him.

I pointed to the *We're Hiring. No Experience Needed.* sign in the window.

"I won't go without you. I mean it," I said.

It's always been easier in our house — my father's house — to stay silent. Easier on the doors, on the windows. On me.

But Mom and I were in this together, and I couldn't let her swim by herself.

He's been talking less and slamming more since I dove in and said, "That's great, Mom. It's a step."

"A step, my ass. What the hell do you know about anything?" was the last full sentence he spoke to either of us.

•

After school I go next door to ask Mrs. B. if she needs more help.

I've known Mrs. B. all my life. I never met either of my grandmothers — Mom's mom died just before I was born, and my father doesn't keep in touch with his mother — but if I had, I'd want them to be like her.

She's moving into a bungalow near my school. "I'm not ready for a retirement village, but my knees sure are. They're worn out from all these stairs," she's fond of saying.

Yesterday I emptied out the crawl space in her basement. The day before, the cold cellar and the furnace room.

"You're a dear," Mrs. B. says when I find her.

She's in her garage, standing beside a jumbled pile of furniture. "It's been growing for years. Who knows what's at the bottom," she says, reaching up and prying free a chair. "Let's tug the whole lot out to the curb."

It's garbage day tomorrow. Mrs. B. says, "One woman's trash is another's treasure." She's left things out before. "You watch. Everything will be long gone by the time the garbage men come by."

We push and pull and carry it all — chairs, picture frames, a coffee table, a dresser — down the driveway.

"Listen to me huffing and puffing," Mrs. B. says.

I'm out of breath too by the time we get to the last piece, a desk wrapped in thick plastic. As we're uncovering it, I hear my father pull into our driveway. I know it's his car, not Mom's, by the way he shuts the door.

*Slam.*

Mom started training on Monday and he's been leaving work early so he can be in the kitchen, opening and closing cupboards, when she walks into the house.

*Slam, slam, slam.*

He likes his dinner to be on the table when he gets home.

Even though her knees may be old, I know there's nothing wrong with Mrs. B.'s hearing, but she doesn't let on that she's heard him. Instead, she puts her hand on the desk and gives it a little pat. "This has been in the family forever," she says.

"Mrs. B., are you sure you want to get rid of it?"

"It's seen better days," she says. So has Mrs. B. Mr. B. ("my Frank" she still calls him) died a couple of years ago. "Let someone else find a good use for it."

We're halfway to the street when, suddenly, I stop and say, "I could use it."

I've always done my homework on the kitchen table, but lately my pencil jumps with every slam.

Mrs. B. and I change direction and we lift it across the grass strip between our houses, over to the stairs by my front door.

"Don't worry, Mrs. B." She knows I'm not just talking about how I'm going to get the desk to my room. "I'll wait here for Mom. She's coming any minute. She'll help me move it."

•

Mom and I are almost at the door when my father opens it. "Don't think that piece of crap is coming into my house."

I guess bringing home the neighbor's trash is enough to get him talking again.

He's standing at the top of the steps, looking down

on Mom and me, and his face is getting redder and redder, and his neck is strained like he's having trouble swallowing.

"Put it in the garage," he spits out.

He's speaking louder than normal.

He looks over at Mrs. B.'s house. He always calls her "the interfering old bitch," but I've never heard her say anything about him. She's only said, "You know my door is always open."

He gets his voice under control, lowers it and says, "The minute she moves, it's out there," he jerks his chin towards the rest of the furniture, "where you should have left it."

*Slam.*

Mom and I take a couple of steps backwards and we set the desk down in the garage beside the garbage pails.

•

After dinner he tells Mom to make coffee. She's pouring it when he says, "Don't work Saturday. A couple of the guys are coming over for a barbecue."

He manages a warehouse and every so often he invites some of the new men who work for him — the chosen few, he calls them — home.

His favorite saying is, "Lead by example."

"And you." I'm trying to do my homework. "Forget the fair. I want you here too."

He takes a sip of coffee and he says, "I can't drink this shit. Too bitter."

He walks over to the sink and dumps his full mug into the dishwater. "What's your boss gonna do when he finds out you can't make a decent cup?"

*Slam.*

It's not only my pencil that jumps. I do too. And so does Mom.

•

On Saturday my father kicks off the charades, starting with Mom and me.

"My wife, Linda," he says. "She hasn't worked since before the kid was born and she's just started back, what's it been, a week now?" He barely glances at Mom, doesn't wait for an answer. "And already they're talking supervisor. That's something, eh?"

I can tell by the way Mom is holding her smile — stretching it, thin, thin, thinner — that this is news to her.

He points his finger at me.

When I was born, Mom wanted to call me Ruby, after her mother, but he said it wasn't Christian enough.

"My daughter, Charity," he says. "Know how I handle those damn dinnertime phone calls? I say, 'I already gave to Charity' and hang up. I don't lie. Never have. Never will."

My smile is hurting my cheeks.

It's not the first time he has said this. But it's the first time this group has heard it.

There's no slamming today. Just a lot of elbow nudging and winking and ha-ha-ha-ing.

He doesn't introduce his guests to Mom and me.

He begins his tour, everyone following behind him, and Mom and I get to fade into the background.

My father is proud of his lawn. Freshly mowed and trimmed. "You let in a few weeds and, before you know it, there goes the neighborhood," he laughs.

"It's all about appearance," he tells them.

In the house he says, "A place for everything."

In the garage, "Everything in its place."

The only thing that looks like it doesn't belong is Mrs. B.'s desk. It's still where Mom and I left it.

One of his chosen few speaks up and says, "Bird's-eye maple! You're not throwing this beaut out, are you? You could get a lot of money for it — two, maybe three thousand bucks."

"Oh, yeah?" my father says.

Then he launches into the subject that's dear to his heart.

"You guys know about 9/11? It was the CIA. You know that? Right?"

He spends the rest of the visit talking about his conspiracy theories, and his flock gobbles them up along with the hot dogs and the coleslaw.

My father brings Mom and me into focus again for the goodbyes. We put our smiles back on and stand beside him on his green lawn — his picture-perfect family — waving.

He says, "Charity, don't worry about the desk. I'll handle it."

I wasn't worried.

Until now.

•

I'm still outside, in front of our open garage, when my father gets home. Mom has gone inside to start dinner, but I stayed to watch the moving truck and Mrs. B.'s car disappear around the corner at the bottom of our street.

It only takes him a second to notice.

"Where is it?" he says, coming towards me.

I make myself speak slowly, calmly, but inside I'm racing. To escape.

"I gave it back. To Mrs. B.," I say.

"You. Did. What?" He's raising his arm, his hand clenching into a fist, I take a couple of steps backwards.

"John," I hear Mom cry. "Don't!"

"What? What?" He drops his arm to his side. I start to tremble. "You think I'd hit her? Hit my own daughter? You think that?" He sounds wounded.

And then he shouts, "You, the both of you, you make me crazy!" And he rushes past Mom.

*Slam.*

And Mom rushes to me.

Even with her holding me, I can't stop shivering.

"Oh, Char, oh, my baby. It's okay," Mom says. I can feel her heart beating as fast as mine. "It'll be okay, I promise."

•

Mom and I pack only one suitcase between the two of us. We don't want to carry too much of this house — his house — to Mrs. B.'s new home. She knows we're coming. "Stay as long as you need to," she said on the phone. She's left her door open.

I want to go right now. "He's watching TV. He won't hear us."

But Mom says, "I have to do this, I'll have to face him sometime. Another step, Char."

He's watching one of his conspiracy shows. This one's about the moon landing, that it never happened, how NASA faked it.

He doesn't say anything when Mom tells him we're leaving, doesn't ask where we're going, doesn't look at us, he just sits in his chair, shaking his head.

Disgusted.

Like we're a big disappointment to him.

Or maybe he's disgusted with Neil Armstrong for going along with the cover-up, disappointed a guy like that lied.

"That's one small step for man ..."

He grabs the controller. Turns the sound up higher.

"... one giant leap for mankind."

And Mom and I turn away and take a couple of steps forward and we're out the door.

I pull it shut behind us.

Softly.

# The Whirlpool

There's no need for Snapchat or text messages in a high school cafeteria at lunchtime. All you have to do is sit at one of the tables. Guaranteed, after a minute or two, you'll know everything there is to know. It's all here. Carried just above our heads. Words surging and swelling and rolling across the cafeteria like bodysurfers at a concert. Talk washing over us, flooding us with the ohmygods, the names, the details. Everyone, even the quiet ones, caught up in the rumors. The gossip. The whirlpool.

Sometimes the whirlpool slows. A sudden waiting, watching, listening silence. A signal that fresh drama is about to unfold. Not on the stage at the back of the room, the curtain drawn shut. This theater plays out right in front of us, on the floor, in the depths of the cafeteria.

I'm not surprised when the current pauses in front of me. It's the end of September, but it's still my name that swirls around and around and around. My name that's been trapped in the whirlpool since school started, the day after Labor Day.

"You're Jasmine. Right?"

I look up from my math homework as a diaper bag and a pretend baby in its carrier are set down, more like plunked, on the empty chair beside me.

"Be a pet and babysit for me until after lunch. K?"

Lindsay. From grade eleven. A year ahead of me. The sweetness of her perfume doesn't match the smile on her lips.

And, so there's no misunderstanding, she adds, "I hear you'll know what to do — for real — if she wakes up."

She doesn't wait for my answer. She shifts her gaze to the girl sitting next to me like she's just noticed her. She widens her smile.

She says, "Ohhhhhh, Julia, always helping the little ones, you're soooooo nice."

Julia, also in grade eleven, on the food-drive committee, on the safe-schools committee, on just about every committee our school has. And my math tutor last year, at the end of grade nine before the final exam.

Julia, who declared herself my friend this year on the second day back at school, when she said, "Hey, you still need some help?" She pointed to the math sheets spread out in front of me, but I knew she was offering me more than help with my homework. At first I was embarrassed, awkward with her, but she didn't seem to care what people thought. Like Poppa, my grandfather, who I live with. So I told her what happened over the summer. I told her about Bella.

Julia stands. She's short. She has to look up at Lindsay but she doesn't blink, not once, as she says, "Thank you, Lindsay. That's soooooo nice of you to say."

I watch as Lindsay's smile falters in the face of nice.

Julia — I think she's the tallest person in the cafeteria right now — waits a couple of seconds. Then, so there's no misunderstanding, she says, "But sorrrrrry, you'll have to find another babysitter, we're leaving."

I don't look at anyone as I follow Julia out of the cafeteria. But I hear the current start up again. Stronger as the whirlpool gorges on the new whispers.

Julia doesn't understand why I won't let her fix this. "Jaz, let me tell a few people. By tomorrow they'll all be talking about someone else."

I don't understand why myself. When school started I figured kids I knew from grade nine would ask me about Bella, but they didn't, their eyes always slipping past mine, never stopping long enough to inquire.

Instead they asked their questions in the cafeteria.

"Why did she leave town last June, as soon as school finished?"

"Why did she disappear for the whole summer?"

"Why were she and her grandfather at the mall on Labor Day at Baby Gap?"

And the whirlpool answered.

"You saw the stroller."

"You saw the baby."

"You know why."

I thought the talk would go away — evaporate — if I kept my head down, ignored it, pretended not to hear. But it didn't go away. It murmured and rippled and bubbled, got stirred around, until it boiled into a new life. Not my life. A new story. Not my story. And I wasn't sure how to stop it. It didn't seem to be mine to stop. I'd been swallowed up. The old Jaz. The one from last year who could sit at a table in the cafeteria, listening. Anonymous. Safe.

Even the teachers were beginning to hear about this new Jaz. They don't spend much time in the cafeteria, so they're always slow to catch on. But this morning, when I handed my test to Miss Finn, she asked me in a hushed voice, "Jasmine, is everything okay with you? Okay at home?"

"Everything is good." My voice lifted up the word *good*. Like a cheerleader. "Give me a *G*, give me an *O*, give me another *O*, give me a *D*. What's that spell? *GOOD*." As much as I like Miss Finn, there was no way I was going to say anything more. Not while my English class listened behind me, their fishing nets out, hoping to snare my answer and feed it to the sharks at first lunch.

As I head towards my last period I pass a group of girls clustered in a circle outside a classroom holding on to their babies. Lindsay's parenting class playing with their dolls. I don't see Lindsay but I know she's there, in the center, tossing her blond ponytail. I imagine them all, silly and giggling, chanting behind me,

"K-I-S-S-I-N-G.
First comes love,
then comes marriage,
then comes baby
in the baby carriage."

And I stand in the crush of the hallway, paralyzed for a moment. Overwhelmed by anger. An anger that twists my stomach, that clenches my fists. This Jaz wants to kick a locker, to throw her voice down the hall. Loud. To shout into Lindsay's classroom. To shout into the cafeteria. To shout, "It doesn't always work that way! Sometimes you just get the baby. In the baby carriage."

But I don't. Instead, I walk past my geography teacher, past the surprised O of his mouth. I walk to the end of the hall and out the door. I walk home, towards Poppa and Bella. I'll give Guidance an excuse to phone. "Sir, Jasmine skipped class today. Oh, and-by-the-way-sir, it's been brought to our attention: your granddaughter is a slut."

The street I live on isn't far from the school. Leafy trees — turning scarlet — line the sidewalk. Lawns are neatly mowed. Small houses are set back from the curb. Windows are closed, shuttered. It's quiet at this time of the afternoon, but even here the whispers follow me. "The apple doesn't fall far from the tree," they say. "Like mother, like daughter."

Poppa doesn't ask me right away why I'm home early. He says, "First I'll make tea." He thinks everything can be solved over a cup of tea — sugar in mine, a splash of Crown Royal in his. He hands me Bella, who is asleep in his arms. I should be comfortable with her by now, but Poppa does most of the holding. She doesn't weigh much more than those pretend dolls at school, but the responsibility of her is heavy. I breathe her in, the baby powder and the pee. The warm-milk smell of her. I carry her into the living room and sit down on the couch, her tiny curled-in-sleep body snuggled safe against me.

The teakettle begins to whistle, startling Bella — her arms suddenly reaching out, her hands suddenly clenching into fists — but she doesn't wake. She curls back into me.

I can't ignore Bella anymore, hoping she'll go away. She's not going anywhere. Not like my mother who gave me my Disney World name.

When Poppa and I came home from a summer at a cottage up north — his retirement gift to us — we found my mom sitting where I sit now, looking at us with empty eyes all drained of fairy-tale endings. She left the next day. She left Bella behind. Like she left me behind twelve years ago.

Poppa raised me. He has fed me, nourished me with a banquet of words since I was three. Words like *pride* and *integrity* and *self-respect*. I used to tease him, call him "Poppa Oprah," but I think of those words now.

And I think of the way Julia stood up to Lindsay today.

And I think of my sister. Cradled and oblivious. For how long?

Sure, Poppa's tea will help, but I already know what I have to do.

Tomorrow, at lunchtime, I'll wade across the cafeteria. I'll keep my head high, my chin above the water, I won't get dragged below by the undertow.

I won't turn away, won't blink.

I'll do this for Bella — one day she'll be thinking of me the way I think of Poppa and Julia — but more, I'll do this for myself.

I will look the whirlpool in the eye.

# OH!

As assembly-line beginnings go, the doll's was no different in any way from the others. Not in shape. Or form. Indeed, hers was a typical molding: plastic pellets melted, hot liquid poured, head, torso, arms and legs cast.

The doll cooled.

And she hardened.

Her pieces were fitted into their sockets and snap-snap-snapped firmly into place.

Her face painted on — precisely sprayed — the colors uniformly premixed.

"Predictably predictable" was the doll maker's motto. "Why tinker? Sales are brisk." Hence a brush of pre-ordained this for her cheeks, a smidgeon and a half darker for her lips, shades of predetermined that for her eyes.

Et cetera.

And, in the corner of each pupil, a tiny star, outlined and filled in as bright as bright can be.

A twinkle.

A glimmer.

A wink to her future.

The doll's hair — her purpose, her raison d'être — machine sewn with absolute care, strand by shiny nylon strand, into her scalp. Meticulously measured and trimmed. Curled. Crimped. Ringleted. Bangs flipped to the side.

Just so.

Gloriously crowned.

And, voilà, there the doll was. A thing of beauty. A joy for some gratefully grateful child. A forever-treasured treasure.

From the top of her preciously coiffed head to the tip of her inflexible little toes, she measured exactly thirteen inches. Exactly identical to the other dolls. Exactly exact, all of them.

There was nothing unusual about her.

While she was being dressed and shoed and

jauntily accessorized — and closely inspected for flaws, turned upside down and every way around — she chit-chatted with her neighbors.

"Oh! Your hair is so perfectly perfect!" the doll said.

"Oh! Your hair is so perfectly perfect!" the doll to her left said.

"Oh! Your hair is so perfectly perfect!" the doll to her right said.

Throughout the factory a chorus of dolls sang out the very same thing.

"Oh! Oh! Oh!"

A harmony of dolly-sweet voices soared aloft, tra-la-la-ing all the way up, up, up to the rusted steel girders high, high, high overhead.

She was placed inside a gilded box. A pre-labeled gilded box stamped in curlicue script — Oh! So Perfect Hair Dolly — the oval *O* in *Oh!* embossed, a foiled mirror, glossily capturing and reflecting the factory fluorescent lights suspended far above her.

Why, it was no wonder the doll believed she alone was under the limelight.

*Oh! Look how those lights shine down on me!*
*Oh!*

She was posed — legs together, feet aligned, one arm at her side, the other reaching forward in anticipation — and fastened to the cardboard back.

Her hair was discreetly taped in place — not one wisp daring to misbehave — beside a comb, a brush, and a plethora of clips and ribbons and bows.

The front of her box was enclosed in cellophane. Sharp corners. Staples unobtrusive. Wrinkles unacceptable.

And, ta-dah, she was ready.

Set.

Go.

Upsy-dolly, she was bundled with the others onto a truck, boxes neatly stacked and secured, bound for the doll shoppe.

As happy-go-luck would have it, she was stowed on the very top. She heard the flustered unfortunates beneath her, fussing and fretting and boo-hoo-hooing.

"Oh! Me!"

"Oh! My!"

"Oh! Dear, the dark!"

"Oh! Oh! Oh!"

Disquieted, she could not raise her arms to cover her tiny ears, so she "oh-me-oh-my-oh-dear'd" along with them.

Until finally, as they were rocked and swayed in the truck's hold, a fitful silence descended with only a muffled "oh!" every mile … then two … then three.

And a low growl from the engine hushed even those.

Lulled under a soft sliver of light escaping from the cab, the doll whiled away the rest of her journey dreaming grand dreams about what would surely soon be.

*Oh! Soon I will greet my child!*

*Oh! Soon I will be instantly loved. Forever. And ever and ever!*

*Oh! Soon I will have my name!*

*Ohhh!*

Only the most loved dolls were named. So, naturally, her most fervent wish was a name. A perfect name. A reflection of her.

Why, what more could she possibly ask for?

*Oh! My name will be my very best accessory!*

*Oh! It will complete my niftily nifty outfit!*

*Oh! What will it be? Adelaide? Beatrice? Celeste?*

The doll lost track of how many times she began the alphabet anew, her name becoming more beautifully beautiful — *Oh! Arabella? Bonnibella? Christabella?* — as she neared her predestination.

The truck arrived at twilight whilst the sky was painted divine shades of indigo. The doll glimpsed it through her cellophane window as she was unloaded and conveyed to the shoppe.

*Oh! Precisely the color of my eyes!*

Then she further noticed a fleck of light in the corner of her vision. A star. As bright as bright can be.

*Oh! Precisely like the stars in my eyes!*
The star twinkled.
*Oh! I wish I may!*
It glimmered.
*Oh! I wish I might!*
A wink to her future, to her name.
*Ohhhhhh!*
The star flickered … it began to move … and, in a blink of an eye (which, of course, she could not) it … disappeared.

Poof. Gone. Just like that.

Perplexed, the doll stared (which, of course, she could). Searching. Beseeching.

*Oh! My star!*
*Oh! My wish!*
*Oh! Come back, please, please, pretty please!*
But the star did not reappear, and full darkness descended.

Swiftly.

As it always does.

And, suddenly, a feeling the doll was not molded to feel hollowed its way into her solid plastic center.

An ache.

As empty as that night sky.

*Oh.*

The single globe light around the back of the shoppe caught her in its moon-shaped beam. The door beneath it opened. She was whisked inside.

In the hustle and bustle that followed, she convinced herself that the peculiar ache was merely the flurry ... the flutter ... the tizzy of it all.

*Oh! Soon, soon, soooooooon!*

By morning she was shelved, in the very center of her aisle, straightened out and properly realigned.

So much so that when the lights were switched on and the doors were unlocked and she heard the quickened steps of the shoppers — the holiday was almost upon them, less than a fortnight away — rushing towards her, the doll was the very first to cry out.

"Oh! Choose me!"

A millisecond's pause ... and a cacophony of voices joined with hers.

"Oh! Choose me. Choose me!"

Throughout the shoppe a discord of dolls cried out the very same thing.

"Oh! Choose me. Choose me. Choose me!"

For that was their way. How else would they be chosen?

"Oh! Oh! Oh!"

A disharmony of dolly-shrill voices caterwauled forth, me-me-me-ing as they practically vibrated themselves right off the shelves. Right into the arms of the next-to-last-minute shoppers.

Arms were mostly all she saw.

Arms reaching above her, below her, across her.
Arms brushing against her.

*Oh! My cellophane! Is that a wrinkle?!*

Willy-nilly mayhem ensued.

Nearly jostled from her perch ... *Oh! Goodness gracious me!* ... she was elbowed back to safety.

She witnessed a not-so-lucky Oh! So Perfect Hair Dolly on the opposite aisle teeter ... totter ... topple.

*Oh! That poor dear!*

*Oh! Her box will be trampled upon, crushed!*

*Oh! She will be banished to the reduced bin!*

For that dreadfully dreadful bin was where damaged dolls were sent. Most languished there forever.

And ever and ever.

Forgotten.

A fate worse than ... there was no worse fate.

*Oh! I will not, will not, will not think of that!*

And ... *Oh! Gosh!* ... she did have more pressing things to think about.

A child loomed in front of her ...

*Oh! This cannot possibly be my child!*

... It leaned in ...

*Oh! What a nest of hair!*

... closer ...

*Oh! Is that jam?!*

... closer ... eyes feverish ... an adult hand appeared and grabbed its jacket collar and ...

*Oh! Phew!*

... dragged it away, its screeches ringing inside her box.

Thus, the day continued. It raced on. Time flew. And so did the dolls, more and more, flying off the shelves.

The doll to her left was chosen.

The doll to her right was chosen.

Dolls above and below and across from her were chosen.

Alas.

She was not.

Chosen.

And for the first time since the previous evening, she felt a twinge of that empty night-sky ache.

*Oh.*

The shopping hordes thinned — hurrying home to check their lists twice — and the shoppe keeper readied for closing: sales tallied, doors locked and bolted, lights dimmed.

In the shadows, preparations were made to welcome the nightly shipment of Oh! So Perfect Hair Dolly dolls.

The doll was shifted off-center, down the aisle a tad, to make room.

*Oh.*

But thank goody-goodness for her, the fresh-from-the-factory dolls disembarked bearing joyous tidings.

"Oh! We are the doll of the year!"

"Oh! There is no stopping us!"

"Oh! We will all be chosen before the holiday!"

"Oh! Oh! Oh!"

The news buoyed her ...

*Oh! Hooray!*

... lifted her spirits ...

*Oh! Hurrah, rah, rah!*

... she was revived ...

*Oh! Tomorrow is another day!*

The doll was not chosen the next day or the next or the next. She was shifted farther down the aisle the next night and the next and the next. But she was not concerned in the least. Why should she be? Her future was for certainly certain.

And besides (why be wrapped up early and hidden away in a closet?) she was enjoying herself immensely.

The camaraderie.

"Oh! You are perfectly perfect exactly the way you are!"

The gossip.

"Oh! Did you see the size of that shopper's basket?!"

Even the moment of remembrance for those in the reduced bin.

"Oh! Thank heavens it isn't me!"

"Oh! Oh! Oh!"

A sign outside the shoppe flashed *Only seven (7!)*

*shopping days left*, and the doll — so fully enthralled by the festivities, merrily fa-la-la-ing along — did not notice the lights inside dimmed darker than usual, the shoppe keeper's whispered instructions, the goings-on across the aisle.

Until she heard a gasp from the doll to her left.

"Oh!"

And a gasp from the doll to her right.

"Oh!"

And gasps from above and below and around her.

"Oh!" and "Oh!" and "Oh!"

"Oh! What is it now? Are we the doll of the decade? The century? The millennium?!" the doll said.

"Oh! No, no, no. There is a new doll in town!" her companions said.

She peered across the aisle. She saw the outline of the boxes. They looked reassuringly familiar.

"Oh! Pishposh. Don't be dotty, nothing is amiss, they are us!" the doll said.

The just-arrived dolls chimed in, enthusiastically agreeing with her ... at first.

"Oh! We are you, exactly exact!"

"Oh! But ... better!"

"Oh! We are a perfectly perfected you!"

"Oh! Oh! Oh!"

The shoppe lights blazed on.

Lo and behold.

The perfectly perfected dolls were revealed.

"One must not rest on one's laurels" was the doll maker's motto. "Strike now! The market is afire." Hence the addition of a beauty-mark heart upon the cheek.

Immediately, the doll pictured her own cheek adorned with a beauty-mark heart.

*Oh! I want, want, want one!*

And then the doll pictured her cheek — as it was — sadly unadorned.

*Oh! Why, why, why did I not get one?*

She managed to keep a stiff upper lip (which, of course, she could).

*Oh! I will not give those upstarts the satisfaction!*

"Oh! Whoop-de-doo. All this hoopla over a teensy-weensy heart?" the doll said.

"Oh! And a new name!" those upstarts said.

She looked more closely and saw Oh! So Perfect and *Lovable* Hair Dolly stamped on their boxes.

The doll was indignant. Outraged. If she could have (which, of course, she could not), she would have furrowed her brow, even if it meant marring her perfectly smooth surface.

"Oh! I. Am. Lovable!" the doll said.

The new dolls tsk-tsked and tut-tutted and told her what was what.

"Oh! No sirree!"

"Oh! You are not!"

"Oh! You are what your box says you are!"

"Oh! Oh! Oh!"

Stunned, she pondered …

*Oh! Not lovable?*

… and pondered …

*Oh! But only the most loved dolls are named.*

… and pondered some more …

*Oh.*

Her perfect dolly world was spinning … dizzily topsy-turvy … What was down? … What was up? … What was uncertain? … What was certain? … What were untruths? … What were … well, the truths were inescapable. They were staring her in the face. She wished she could close her eyes (which, of course, she could not).

"Oh. My heart is broken."

The doll did not know she had spoken aloud until she heard a peal of giggles and twitters and tee-hee-hees.

"Oh! You silly you!"

"Oh! Your heart cannot be broken!"

"Oh! You have no heart. Only we do!"

"Oh! Oh! Oh!"

Touché.

That empty night-sky ache, it hollowed deeper. And deeper. And deeper. Her solid plastic center was cracking open, exposing her doubts.

*Oh. Who am I, if not named?*
*Oh. Merely perfect.*
*Oh. Like every other doll.*
*Oh.*
*Ohhh.*
*Ohhhhhh.*
The doll tried to speak.
She choked.
The remaining Oh! So Perfect Hair Dolly dolls dared ask what she could not.
"Oh! But what of us?"
They needn't have worried.
"Everyone appreciates a pre-holiday sale" was the shoppe keeper's motto. "Win-win. Ka-ching!" Hence a half-price sticker slapped onto the Oh! So Perfect Hair Dolly boxes.
And the shoppe opened, and business resumed, and the dolls cried, "Oh! Choose me! Choose me! Choose me!" as was their wont.
Dismayed, the doll discovered she could no longer speak those words.
The dolls on both sides of the aisle were concerned — 'twas the season after all for cheer, goodwill and peace — so they urged her to speak up.
"Oh! Stop your dolly lollygagging or you will not be chosen!"

But try, try, try as she might, each time, the empty night-sky ache silenced her.

By the eve of the holiday — as prophesied, the shoppers were frantic — every single doll had indeed been chosen, even the damaged ones in the bin.

Except her.

She was the last doll left.

She had come to the very end of her aisle, had nowhere to go.

"Out with the old and in with the new" was the shoppe keeper's motto. "No time for niceties. My feast awaits." Hence she was tossed into the reduced bin.

The doll landed with a slamming … jarring … box-damaging … thud.

And there she lay.

Window-side down.

Alone.

She ached. From her fall. From her uncertainties. From the overwhelming doom and gloom at the bottom of the bin.

*Oh. What to do? What to do? What to do?*

"Oh. Hello?"

"Oh. Anyone?"

Her voice echoed weakly inside her box. It was her only answer.

"Oh. Help."

No one came to her rescue.

*Oh. What now? What now? What now?*

She sought to calm herself with the familiar ...

*Oh. Arabella. Bonnibella. Christabella.*

... but by the end ...

*Oh. Xellabella. Yayabella. Zuzubella.*

... the names did not ring true anymore.

*Oh. What else? What else? What else?*

There was nothing else.

And so, the doll had no choice but to do and think and feel ... nothing.

*Oh. Nothing, nothing, nothing, nothing, nothing, nothing, nothing, nothing, nothing, nothing, nothing, nothing, nothing, nothing, nothing, nothing, nothing, nothing, nothing, nothing, nothing, nothing, nothing, nothing, nothing ...*

It was easier that way.

*Oh. Nothing, nothing, nothing, nothing, nothing, nothing, nothing, nothing, nothing, nothing, nothing, nothing, nothing, nothing, nothing, nothing, nothing, nothing, nothing, nothing, nothing, nothing, nothing, nothing, nothing ...*

Comforting.

Almost.

*Oh. Nothing, nothing, nothing, nothing, nothing, nothing, nothing, nothing, nothing, nothing, nothing, nothing, nothing, nothing, nothing, nothing, nothing, nothing,*

*nothing, nothing, nothing, nothing, nothing, nothing, nothing, nothing, nothing, nothing, nothing ...*

Days?

Weeks?

Months?

A year?

She had no way of knowing. Time blurred inside nothing ... nothing ... nothing.

And then, one day, the doll was pulled from nothingness. Startled into somethingness. She found herself gazing into the bright, unblinking eyes of a child.

A jolt of recognition.

*Oh.* **My** *child.*

An oh-so-perfect moment.

But oh so momentary.

Because moments always are.

"She is damaged. Look at these, they have hearts," the parent said.

The child blinked.

And returned the doll to the bin, though propping her up against the wired side, so she could look out.

Look out as the child crossed the aisle.

Look out as the child stood in front of the Oh! So Perfect and Lovable Hair Dolly dolls.

Decisions ...

Look out as the Oh! So Perfect and Lovable Hair Dolly dolls vied for the child's attention.

"Oh! Choose me, me, me!"

"Oh! Oh! Oh!"

Decisions ... decisions ...

Even then, in silenced anguish, the doll could not help noting the child's tidy hair — each strand in its proper place.

Look out as the child began to muss those strands, confusing them. Curling and twirling and twisting. Tangling. Worrying them into knots.

Decisions ... decisions ... decisions ...

The doll thought of her own hair. Her perfect hair — still not one wisp misbehaving — her glorious crown.

Her purpose.

Her raison d'être.

*Oh.*

*Ohhh.*

*Ohhhhhh.*

The empty night-sky ache could no longer silence her.

Au contraire, it assisted her.

**"Oh."**

Fueled and propelled her.

**"You."**

Gave her courage to speak up loud and clear.

**"I. Choose. You."**

"Oh! Shush up. That is not our way!" the other dolls said.

"That is my way," the doll said.

Watching.

As the child turned.

As the child stared.

As the child's eyes widened.

"Which one do you want?" the parent said.

"This one. I need her," the child said.

And, with that, the doll was freed from the bin, whisked through the shoppe, conveyed outside and bundled into an awaiting car.

Safely secured in the backseat, the child tore the cellophane open, unfastened and untaped the doll, and discarded the gilded box — the comb, the brush, and the plethora of clips and ribbons and bows left untouched — on the floor.

And, voilà, there the doll was — exactly where she chose to be, her destination — on the child's lap.

The doll's hardened plastic toes and fingers dug into the child. But the child did not seem to mind as she played with the doll's hair. Curling and twirling and twisting. Tangling the shiny nylon strands.

A tiny knot formed in the doll's hair.

Binding the child and the doll.

Together.

Neither noticed the sun shining, glancing off the rearview mirror. The doll only had eyes for the child, and the child only had eyes for the doll.

"How is she?" the parent said.

The child hugged the doll.

Tight.

Tighter.

So tight, the child's steady heartbeat enveloped her.

"She's perfect."

"Does she have a name?"

"Hairdolly. Her name is Hairdolly!"

And, suddenly, a feeling the doll was not molded to feel burst its way into her cracked plastic center.

A love.

Filling up her empty night-sky ache.

As full as that beat-beat-beating heart.

*OH!*

"A thing of beauty is a joy for ever:
Its loveliness increases; it will never
Pass into nothingness; but still will keep"
– from "Endymion" by John Keats

# A Beautiful Smile

Oh, **geez**.

What **is** this place? This … this … nightmare of a wilderness I've been — thank you, Mom and Dad, thanks a lot — pushed into.

I don't know the rules here …

*412 … 433 … 451 …*

I've lost my bearings …

*469 … 487 … 499 …*

There are no familiar markers to help me find my way …

*513 … 529 … 545 …*

No north-star compass to navigate me down this hard and shiny-surfaced windowless labyrinth — harshly lit from above, no horizon in sight.

It's the longest hall I've ever seen.

And it's ice-jam packed.

I cling to one side, the left side, as close to the wall as possible, gingerly traversing around lockers gaping open, around knapsacks tossed to the floor, around students calling out to each other.

No one calls out to me.

No one knows me.

Me? I'm Nicky. I've just moved to Toronto from the north.

And I'm not talking about the let's-go-for-a-Sunday-drive-outside-the-city north. Not **that** north, pale and dull.

**I. Am. Nicola.**

From **the** north. The far north. My true tundra north, **strong** and **free**.

Like me.

And I'm spirited too — hey, a girl needs a little spark, some fire in her veins, when it's fifty below.

Back home I knew the rules, knew how to survive in the bush. It's legend in my family, the night last winter when I woke with a tingling start. *Warning!* The hair on my arms was already at attention before I saw a wolf crouched on top of my sister's rabbit hutch

— I **told** her that was a dumb place for it — staring yellow-eyed hungry through our bedroom window. At **me**. I **knew** what to do.

Hear me roar!

Only I'm not roaring now. Or strong. Or free to be me. And my northern-spirit self has flown the coop, gone south.

Deserted me, the coward.

When Mom drove me to school this morning, she said, "You'll be fine, just be yourself."

Easy for you to say, Mom. You haven't been cruelly uprooted and dropped into this … this … concrete wasteland, no soft muskeg to cushion the landing. You and Dad **chose** to move here. I swear I'll scream — louder than I have been — if I hear "it's where the jobs are" one more time.

I wish my parents could see me now. Whimpering to myself, cowering and sneaking … seek … *597* … seek … *616* … seeking … *629* … searching for my locker.

In my old school there were no lockers. Just hooks in the foyer where we hung our jackets, two or three on top of each other, boots jumbled on the floor below.

Right now, I'd give anything — no, **everything** — for a whiff of that cramped entryway. That eau de toilette. That heady, steamy Canada-goose-down-stinky-feet, familiar, oh-so-comforting heart-note scent.

Here, in this wild corridor with no end, I'm over-taken, overrun, overwhelmed.

Suffocated by the perfumes and the aftershaves and the body sprays. By the heavy bottom-note, industrial-strength Mr. Clean.

When I signed in at the office — was that **only** a few minutes ago? — the secretary handed me my schedule, and then she cracked a you-poor-girl-you-won't-last-till-lunch pity smile and pointed me out the door towards my doom. And present gloom.

"Your homeroom's 8E, thataway, so's your locker, 711, through the cafeteria, turn left, turn right, go straight. Good luck."

Homeroom?

In my old school I had one teacher. There was one class of grade eights.

Nineteen of us.

In my old school I knew everyone's first name and everyone's last name. I knew their middle initial, if they had one. I knew their sisters and brothers. Their mothers and fathers. I **knew** them.

*687 ...*

I'm getting warmer.

*699 ...*

And warmer.

*705 ...*

Almost there.

What the …?

I look down at my hand, where I red-inked 711 — the magic number. Find my locker, find myself. That's what this epic journey has become.

The 7 has smudged into the 1s a bit — everyone nervous sweats, right? — but, even in this unnatural light, it's clear enough.

I look up.

Up, down, all around confused, I don't know what I'm looking for anymore.

But I know what I'm looking **at**. There's a girl, her back to me, in front of **my** open locker.

This puzzle of a maze — this hall, this school, this city, my new life — has become too much for me to solve on my own.

I tap the girl on the shoulder and say, "Excuse me."

She turns towards me — slow, slow, slowly — and I notice her hair moves with her. Dark and long and silky sleek.

Then the girl smiles and I remember what else Mom said. After she told me I'd be fine. After she told me to be myself. As I was getting out of the car, she said, "And smile, Nicky. You have a **beautiful** smile."

I **do** have a beautiful smile — sorry, Mom, for slamming the door on your advice — and the proof's in my old yearbooks. Always under my picture, the same words: *Voted best smile, melts permafrost.*

So I stand before her with my arm outstretched and my palm open like I'm offering her a gift — so she can also see the number 711 — and I smile and say, "I think this is my locker."

The girl smiles wider (maybe she'll be my friend) and wider (maybe she'll show me the way in this strange Toronto land).

Maybe she'll tell me what shampoo she uses.

And suddenly my arm hairs are rising, tingling, *warning*!

Too late.

If only I hadn't forgotten to pack my trusty survival instincts. Along with my backbone.

The girl's smile has curled all the way back to expose some very pointy incisors. I thought everyone in this city had their own personal orthodontist … no?

She says, "You **think**?"

I don't know **what** to think.

Where I come from wolves are wolves, and girls — even the bitchy ones — are … girls. **Just** girls.

But here, stiff legged and menacingly tall in her platform heels, is clearly a snarling wolf dressed in girls' clothing. A very glossy and fashionable wolf, showing way more skin than a black fly could handle at one sitting.

This … this … she-wolf narrows her eyes and glares me back a couple steps, forcing me out of the shadows, away from the safety of the wall, into the middle of the hall. Startled, I drop my binder, my schedule, my dignity.

The sound echoes off the lockers. Heads turn. A pack of students gather around us.

"Fight!"

*Please, please, please, don't let them smell my fear.*

This might not be the most opportune time to re-call how my only other encounter with a wolf ended. When that one last winter was crouched on top of my sister's rabbit hutch, salivating and ready to pounce, I **did** roar.

All the way to my parents' bedroom.

It was Bernie, four years younger, forty years braver, or so the family joke goes — ha-ha, not funny — who stood on a chair and banged her fist against the window.

I wish Mom and Dad and Bernie were here to pro-tect me now.

But I stand alone, shivering — can I make myself any smaller? — pinned to the spot by this ... this wolf girl's cold, cold, **biting**-cold eyes. Pitiless.

Back home I never felt the chill. Not even in the throes of a raging blizzard.

I'd heard it's a different kind of cold in Toronto but I didn't understand what that meant until this very moment.

Her icy stare begins at my feet and moves upwards. Nothing escapes her. My boots, my jeans, my flannel shirt, my toque.

Some people might call my look lumberjack, but back home my friends and I called it "Northern Chic." Plaid's always in style ... eh?

Obviously not.

Her yellow-ringed irises — why, oh why, didn't I notice the color before? I could have saved myself this humiliation — zero in on my still-outstretched hand. As I'm thinking, *This can't possibly get any worse*, she tilts her head back, baying at the ceiling tiles, "I don't trust a girl with **sweaty** hands."

The whole school, I'm certain, can hear her howl.

I'm losing the battle — *I will not wipe my hands on my pants, I will not, will not* — when there's a commotion behind us. Distracted, she looks away from me and spies bigger and better prey.

**Delicious**-looking prey.

He's separated himself from the crowd and he's walking towards us.

She says, "Jaaaack!"

She's toned it down a notch, made it more sing-songy, but her howl still has a hungry ring to it.

This Jack doesn't look too thrilled to be her morning snack. He says, "Robin."

Robin? A little tweeting birdie? **That's** her name? I was expecting something more … well … wolfish … like … Raven.

Jack's lack of enthusiasm doesn't throw Robin-not-Raven off her game. She circles around him, like she's marking her territory.

She ignores me. I guess I've been … dismissed.

Dismissed?

The way I see it, I have two choices.

I can slink off, tail between my legs, to the nearest bathroom and wash the smeared ink off my sweaty hands. And while I'm there I can check out the stalls, pick which one I'm going to eat lunch in, huddled, hiding out. For the rest of my life. Eww.

**Or**, I can make myself proud.

True north girl, strong and free.

So I take a leap of faith — fingers crossed I won't be frozen out twice — and I reach out again. I grab on to Jack's arm and I smile my beautiful permafrost-melting smile and I say, "Jack!"

And I pull him close, close (ohhhhh), closer.

I've **never** gotten **this** up close and personal at first glance before but … desperate times …

*Please play along with me. Pleeeeeease!*

Whoa! It's true what they say! The eyes **are** the window to the soul. I can see all the way into Jack's heart, and it doesn't need melting. And those eyes! They remind me of home, of the northern lights, shimmering and dancing. Warm.

Robin is spitting ice.

She says, "You ... **you** know Jack?"

My answer is measured. And quiet. Only the three of us can hear. "You. Don't. Know. **Jack,**" I say.

I wait — *one, two, three* — and add, "Like I know Jack."

And then Jack picks up my binder and my schedule from the floor and he looks at my name, typed in block letters across the top, and he says, "Nicola! C'mon, we have the same homeroom."

And I gather up my dignity, and we walk away from Robin.

Dismissed!

I **could** finish her off — turn around and give her a na-na-na-na-na look — but, where I come from, we have a rule: kill only what you'll eat.

And I'm a vegetarian.

# The Sunflower

I do not pay his kind much notice — except to keep the distance between us wide — but his face, with its deep lines and furrows, brought to mind the walnut, a food I greatly treasure.

Food. My precious stores depleted, forever in need of replenishment. It is food I take notice of.

And so.

That morning, from my vantage outside my home, I paused to watch him approach.

His spine was hunched. His gait held no trace of the scamper of youth. Rather, it was slow and deliberate.

He was further weighed down by a chair he carried under one arm.

He did not stray from the path, did not glance about. He had the look of one who knew where he was heading.

He halted just beyond the shade cast from my tree, unfolded his chair and lowered himself into it.

And there he sat, looking straight ahead, squinting into the sun.

I followed his gaze to a newly placed gravestone.

I do not pay gravestones much notice either. I have existed amongst them for most of my life, but they mean nothing. My kind do not bury their dead.

The etchings on this one were gibberish to me, though I recognized the flower that was carved into it.

The sunflower. Another treasured food.

Food. Winter scarcities not fully forgotten, my belly gnawing at me, I left in search of spring's promise.

I wasted no more thought on him until I returned late in the day to find him on his knees, his head bowed. I have seen his kind do this often enough, but he did not remain idle like the others.

I edged along a branch, curious, and discovered him digging with his fingers, burrowing. Into each hole he dropped a seed. A sunflower seed.

Food.

I waited.

Finally, he patted the earth and stood up, reaching for the gravestone to steady himself. He folded his chair and departed.

In a flash, headfirst, I was down my tree.

Food. It consumes me, and I consume it. Furiously, I dug up the treasure he had buried. I feasted on the seeds.

He returned the next day and the next and the next. He tidied the empty shells I left scattered about the gravestone and planted new seeds.

I grew less wary of him. One day, I was halfway to the ground before he stood up.

He spoke.

"They were her favorite flowers. She said they filled a room with sunshine."

I froze and flattened myself against the trunk, inching around to the side farthest from him.

But his voice followed.

"She filled me with sunshine."

My kind are solitary. We do not bond for life. When it was time to go forth from Mother's home, I went.

Brother and I, we leaped together, chasing the sun and each other through backyards to a road. We dashed across. Cars roaring close. Too close. I darted back. I ran. Ran until those fearsome sounds were muffled, finally stopping under this very tree. I looked about. Brother was not with me.

I was alone.

No, we did not speak the same language, he and I, but still, I understood. After that day, I left his seeds where he had planted them.

And each day he left a pocketful of seeds behind for me.

Spring passed.

Summer too.

He sat and watched his sunflowers grow bigger and bigger. He did not speak again.

I kept my distance, but that distance grew smaller and smaller as I watched him watch his sunflowers grow.

Fall arrived and, one morning, he did not. And that was that.

And this was this. Leaves were already slipping from trees, rustling, whispering, warning me to get busy.

Food.

I sprang atop the gravestone. Sheared his sunflowers off the stem. Took them. I buried the seeds.

My kind do not dwell on those who once were. What purpose would it serve? Lingering cannot nourish, cannot fill up an empty gut.

And yet.

I am awake.

In this darkest hour before light — as chill clutches at me and food does not quell my hunger — I curl myself up, wrap my tail closer around me.

I remember.

I remember leaping into the sun.

I remember my joy mirrored in Brother's eyes.

I remember how we soared.

# Destiny

The bus station has an in-the-center-of-a-February-snowstorm feel to it. Even the bit of silver tinsel stuck with masking tape above the Exit sign looks deserted. Lost its flashy cheer. As though it knows it's been abandoned up there, with nobody bothering to take it down after Christmas, it barely stirs each time the automatic door below slides open.

I'm leaning forward in the chair, trying to catch what the announcer on the radio is saying. Something about us outshooting them ten to three and it's only halfway through the first period. Trying to follow the wave of his voice, rising and falling, as he calls out the play. Frig. I think we just scored but I'm not sure.

The radio is over on the counter where the bus tickets are sold. There's only one ticket seller on duty and she's staring dull-eyed (at nothing as far as I can tell) through the grime-streaked glass. Seriously. Would it kill her to pick up a bottle of Windex?

She looks about as interested in the game as the pigeons are, pecking at the scuffed tiles by my feet.

I can't believe she's not listening. It's the Olympics, for crying out loud. Women's hockey.

Maybe she won't mind if I ask her to turn up the volume a bit. I decide against it when I see how her mouth is set — miserable like the weather. Instead I move a couple of rows closer. There's plenty of identical bolted-to-the-floor, butt-numbing, faded (oh, there's a surprise) seats to choose from.

At least I can hear more clearly now: the sticks slapping the ice, skate blades carving, the whack of the puck banging off the boards, the thud as it's stopped by the goalie's glove. And the announcer's voice surging with roller-coaster excitement. "Ohhhhhhhhh, what a save."

For a second I wish I were back at the restaurant watching the game on TV.

But then I rub the charm that hangs from the chain around my neck. A shiny silver circle, kept polished bright by my fingertips. I don't need to look down to read the words engraved on it. FOLLOW YOUR HEART. Turn it over and it says, THE PATH TO YOUR DESTINY.

Destiny.

Well.

I'm on the path.

One day I'll play in goal for Canada. Wear the red-and-white jersey at the Olympics. Go for gold. It feels right to be here, today, at this moment, in this bus station, listening to the game.

If I were my uncle, my mother's brother, I'd be buying a lottery ticket at that United Cigar Store over there by the main entrance. Uncle Jimmy's always looking for a sign. "Dani, how many shots you stop last night?" Always looking for his lucky number. "Twenty-nine? Then that's my lucky number, that's the number that's gonna make me rich."

But I'm not my Uncle Jimmy. I know it takes more than luck to win. I don't leave destiny to chance.

I didn't learn to play hockey in an arena. I learned in the parking lot behind my parents' restaurant. Johnny taught me. Always the big brother, having to look after me while Mom and Dad were busy getting ready for the dinner rush. Every day at four, I watched Johnny practice his slap shot, aiming for the fence built to hide the garbage bins, leaving deep dents in the wood.

My brother finally got tired of me whining — "It smells out here, I'm cold, Johnny, I wanna go in" — so he made me goalie. He put a stick in my hand and a couple of pylons on either side of me, and he called out advice like, "Keep the stick on the ground, Dani, so you're ready," and "Don't look at me, Dani, keep your eyes on the puck," and "Don't be scared, Dani, use everything you've got, make yourself big."

I don't know who was more thrilled the first time I stopped the puck. Me or Johnny. "Way to go, Dani, way to go." And then after a few more saves, I remember Johnny shouting through the back door of the restaurant, "Come outside. Come watch Dani play. She's smart, she knows where I'm aiming before I do."

And my father appearing, standing at the back door, apron tied around his waist, holding a wooden spoon in one hand. Holding on to the old ways. Lifting the spoon up to punctuate his words, he said, "Girls don't play hockey."

Period.

End of story.

He'd already started to turn away, his spoon still up in the air, when my brother spoke. Even back then, Johnny was the biggest kid on his hockey team. A man's body. With a boy's voice. Soft. Respectful. That day, it carried clean across the parking lot. Turned our father around.

"She's a natural, Dad. You watch, one day she'll be a better hockey player than me."

And me, standing behind my defender, almost as tall as my brother — the regulars always asking, "What do you feed these two?" — looking at Dad over Johnny's shoulder.

Me, steaming.

Thank you very much, big brother.

But.

I can fight my own battles.

Me, stepping out from Johnny's shadow, lifting my stick above my head, jabbing it up and down three times, three exclamation marks. What is it with Dad and me and punctuation?

I knew, right then and there, in that parking lot, that I was declaring my destiny.

"Yeah, you watch me, I'm gonna kick hockey ass one day."

I wasn't the only one on dish duty that night. Mom made Uncle Jimmy scrub the pots too.

"Whaaat? What'd I do?"

"Where'd Dani learn that word? From listening to you. That's where."

So.

I knew hockey was my destiny.

But Dad didn't.

The next day he took me to the arena across the street from the restaurant and signed me up for figure-skating lessons. He pointed to the sequined skaters (who the heck sews all those tiny things on?) gliding by us, sparkly and graceful.

He said, "This is for girls."

I kept my mouth shut. No way was I going to argue with him — a goalie needs to know how to skate.

Even if she has to learn with toe picks.

And I learned, all right. Better than all right. I passed some levels, brought home some badges, pleased Dad.

"That's my girl!"

He told me to invite Debbie, my coach, to the restaurant for dinner. The night she showed up, we were jam-packed, no tables available.

From behind the counter, where I was scrounging for food, I watched the puck drop and the game begin.

I remember Mom gesturing with her thumb.

"Out."

And Uncle Jimmy gracefully — "Okay. Okay." — sacrificing his favorite table for Debbie.

The table across from the two chalkboards. One chalkboard for the daily specials and one chalkboard — the one Jimmy had his eye on — keeping count of Johnny's goals.

Dad waltzing — chin high and shoulders squared (Debbie would approve), chest pumped full of pride — out of the kitchen with a pan of saganaki.

"Welcome!"

Debbie talking me up, making me blush (or maybe it was the hot peppers I was eating). "Dani's edge control ... strength ... agility ... no one at the rink can beat her for speed."

Dad, his timing perfect, lighting the saganaki with his signature flourish — "Opa!" — the cheese flaming and sizzling. Everyone oohing and aahing. Dad's face glowing.

Then Dad sprinkling the lemon juice, the flame dying down, the cheese cooling, the restaurant suddenly quiet.

And Debbie, breaking the silence, saying, "But she needs to focus on other skills too ... jumps, spins, spirals."

Me — my mouth full — sputtering.

"I'm not wasting my ice time on any of that fancy crap."

Debbie, scoring the clincher in overtime.

"Mr. Stavros, have you ever considered putting Dani in hockey?"

I'm certain I heard the air escaping from Dad's deflating chest. *Hissssssssssss*. I think the whole restaurant heard it.

The next day he took me to Canadian Tire and traded my figure skates in for hockey skates. I remember my feet sliding right into them. They fit me way better.

"And I need pads and gloves and a helmet too. With a face mask, a goalie needs a real good mask," I said.

"And you gotta register me in house league. Boys house league."

And Dad, both hands in the air, looking up at the ceiling — I don't know if he was talking to himself or to the sales guy or to God — saying, "What you gonna do?"

My point.

Exactly.

Maybe Dad wasn't happy about the way I was outfitted. But Johnny was. He didn't have to hold back on his shots against his practice goalie anymore. And I learned — quickly — how to best avoid dents in my new equipment.

This year Johnny's playing in the Ontario Hockey League. My brother hasn't scored any goals yet — "He's still settling in," Dad says — but he's the kind of guy who always shows up ready to work hard, to help his team get the job done.

Like I do.

If anyone is paying attention.

Helllllo ... Olympics ... red-and-white jersey ...

I reach for my charm, give it a rub. Not because I'm expecting a genie to magically appear and grant me my wish. But because it reminds me why I'm here. Today. Waiting for a bus.

Destiny.

Johnny's first choice was the Oshawa Generals. So he could stay closer to home. Home being the restaurant, more home to us than the house where we sleep. Mom wanted Oshawa too. Dad's dream was the Soo Greyhounds, the same team his hero, Wayne Gretzky, played for back when he was becoming a star.

If it were me — if the OHL came knocking on my door? — I wouldn't have a first choice. Or a second or a third. I'd go anywhere.

But.

I'm just a girl.

And when the knock came, we were — where else? — at the restaurant, waiting for the big phone call. I remember Dad and Johnny at the counter, rolling out the phyllo, chopping the spinach, crumbling the feta, making their spanakopita. Mom writing out the specials on the chalkboard. Me talking about — what else?

"The Leafs are never gonna win the Cup if they don't —"

And then the phone ringing and me diving for it and handing it to Johnny, and Dad saying, "Which one? Which one?" and me saying, "I don't know, I don't know," and Mom saying, "Shhhh, shhhh," and Johnny covering his other ear with his hand and twisting slightly away from us, and saying, "yes" and "no" and "yes" and "thank you" and hanging up.

And Johnny turning back towards us, saying, "I got drafted" like he couldn't quite believe it.

And Dad and Mom and me saying, "By who?" Shouting, "Whoooo?"

"The Soo."

Sault Ste. Marie's a ten, maybe eleven-hour bus ride from here. My parents argued over Johnny playing so far away. Too far to come home much. This is how the argument went. Mom said, "He's too young, maybe he should wait until he's finished school."

Dad said, "Gretzky was the same age, sixteen."

The night before Johnny left, he and Dad cooked up a feast. The restaurant was crammed fuller than my hockey bag, with family and friends and customers.

I remember my brother serving his special keftedes and the regulars stage-whispering, "Your old man can't cook like this, we'll starve when you're gone!"

Aunt Melina, my mother's sister, asking, "Daniela, when are you gonna learn how to cook?"

Me too busy stuffing my mouth full of the meatballs — hey, a girl works up an appetite playing hockey like I do. Mom answering for me, "Why would she? When she has two men cooking for her?"

Dad pouring the ouzo. "First the OHL. Then the NHL. You'll break Gretzky's record, eh, Johnny?"

Dad raising his glass, "My son, the next Great One."

And Johnny on his way back to the kitchen — ducking the spotlight at center ice — saying, "Dad, I play defense, not offense."

My father lifting his shoulders. "Offense. Defense." Giving his these-are-minor-details shrug.

The whole family was here, at the bus station, to say goodbye. Some of the regulars too. A hero's sendoff. Uncle Jimmy was saying, "Look at that, Johnny. It's a sign. You're on a Greyhound bus goin' up to play for the Soo Greyhounds. I'm winning the lottery tonight."

The lottery.

That's what people think Johnny won, making it to the OHL. Everyone at the restaurant, at the arena, at school always saying, "How's Johnny?" More a high five than a question, no one expecting an answer.

No one except my teacher, Mr. Rogers. He's asked me a couple of times and the way he asks, it's like he's really interested in knowing.

"He's living the hockey dream, Mr. Rogers, he's living the dream."

Seriously.

What else is there to say?

Or so I thought.

And then, yesterday, Mr. Rogers gives us this assignment: write a letter you'll never mail.

He said, "If you think no one's going to read it, it'll free you up. Say something you've been dying to say. Dig deep. You'll dig up the truth."

None of us bothered to point out that Mr. Rogers would be reading our letters. He's the kind of teacher you don't mind digging up the truth with.

Anyway, at the end of the class, I'm walking past him and he asks again, "How's Johnny?" and I'm almost out the door when — puck shot to the head — it hits me.

Johnny must have written the same assignment back when he was in Mr. Rogers' class. He wrote a letter he'd never send and Mr. Rogers read it.

And Mr. Rogers knows something about my brother that I don't.

Johnny and I have always done our homework at the restaurant, on the computer in the corner of the kitchen. The letter wasn't hard to find. All I did was click on Saved Documents. And — bingo! — there it was.

Johnny's truth.

*Dear Dad,*

*As long as I can remember you've talked to Dani and me about destiny. How we have to follow our hearts to find it. Well, I know where my heart is. And I know my destiny too. We share more than a first name. Like Mom says, we're cut from the same cloth, you and I. One day — more than anything, more than the NHL — I want to be your partner, cook beside you, at the restaurant we both love.*

*And, Dad, I need to tell you this: Wayne Gretzky is your hero, not mine.*

*You're my hero.*

*Love, Johnny*

Of course there was more to the letter than that — Johnny padded it with a couple of Dad's and his favorite recipes. You don't get away with one hundred words, not with Mr. Rogers — believe me, I've tried — but it was those words that rebounded off the screen.

Blindsiding me.

"What the eff?"

I didn't realize I'd spoken out loud until I heard Mom's warning. "Dani."

Mom's still on a mission to clean up my language but before she could say "pots," I was through the back door with my hockey stick in my hand. I don't think straight without it.

Outside, I took aim at the fence hiding the garbage bins.

One shot.

The restaurant over hockey?

Two shots.

He's crazy.

Three shots.

Is that why, every single night, he phones to ask what the specials are?

I stood there, looking at all those deep dents in the wood. Mine and Johnny's. I couldn't tell them apart, they were so mixed up together.

I reached for my charm.

Held on to it.

Destiny.

And, suddenly, standing in the exact spot back when I faced Dad and declared mine, I understood.

I understood that my destiny was not my brother's destiny.

I understood that it was time for Johnny to declare his.

And I understood that Dad would come around.

Eventually.

Because he understands destiny. The charm around my neck? Dad had the first two made, for himself

and Mom, when they got married. And then one for
Johnny when he was born. And this one for me. And,
he understands that, sometimes, destiny needs a little
push.

After all, his mother, my YiaYia, pushed him across
a whole ocean when Mom and her family came to
Canada.

"Go. With Helena. She is your destiny," YiaYia said.

Anyway, last night I phoned my brother — yeah, it's
called interference. So send me to the penalty box. I told
him I read his letter. Said I was sorry before he could
give me shit. I told him to get himself on the next bus.
"Come home and talk to Dad," I said. "Your coach'll let
you, Johnny. You don't have a game until Sunday."

And then I told Mom and Dad he was coming
home for a couple of days. But not why. That was up
to Johnny, his story to tell.

And this morning, before I left to meet him, I
wrote (my mouth already watering) *Johnny's famous
keftedes* on the daily specials chalkboard.

The chalkboard that hangs on the wall across from
Uncle Jimmy's favorite table. In between two other
chalkboards. One keeping count of the goals Johnny
has scored. And one keeping count of the pucks I've
stopped.

The last one up there since that day Dad took me to
Canadian Tire to trade in figure skates for hockey gear.

I remember Dad leaving me in the checkout line
— "Gotta get something for the restaurant" — and
coming back with it.

Dad putting it in our cart.

Dad saying, "Why not, eh?"

And, hey, it's not like it's been smooth skating from
that moment on. I've tripped and crashed into the
boards lots of times. Who doesn't? But I learned this
from my parents, whose first two restaurants failed:
I'm always gonna get up and go after that puck.

The ticket seller's awake now and she's fiddling
with the knobs on the radio. She hasn't tuned in to
anything but static so far, but it doesn't matter. The
bus I've been waiting for is pulling into the station. A
Greyhound bus from the Soo.

I put my notebook and pencil back in my knapsack.
I've finished writing Mr. Rogers' assignment. It's due
tomorrow. My letter is addressed to my big brother. It's
about why (even though we're pretty much the same
height now) I'll always look up to him. And, you know
what? No disrespect, Mr. Rogers, but why write a letter that no one (but you) will read? I'm gonna mail it.

As Johnny walks in, the sliding door stays open
long enough for the icy wind to lift up that lonely bit
of tinsel stuck above the Exit sign. A returning hero's
welcome.

# Book of Dreams

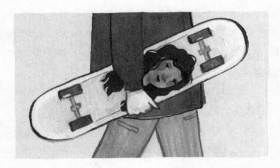

"It's a freakin' ad, kid, an ad for Maple Leaf Turkey," Dave says, shaking his head, crushing my picture into a ball and tossing it behind the TV.

I'm stretched out on the couch watching television, my hood up over my head, not letting on that I care. I don't know why he sounds so pissed off. Maybe it's because he doesn't see himself in the picture. Mom walks into the room, takes a swallow from Dave's beer.

"You know what he wants?" Dave points in my direction with the neck of his beer bottle. "A turkey. Your kid wants a friggin' turkey."

Mom laughs when Dave speaks, but she's not listening to him. By the light of the TV, she's looking around for her cigarettes.

"See ya around, turkey." Now Dave's laughing out in the hall. My mom laughs again and I hear the doors to the elevator shut.

I don't know why I showed it to him. I've never shown it to anyone. Maybe because it's the season, you know, Christmas. Maybe because Dave's been around longer than most of them. Or, maybe because he was the first one to ask.

"Hey, kid. If you could have anything, anything in the world, what would you ask for?"

I carefully smooth out my picture, a page I tore from a magazine I found in some waiting room a long time ago. The creases along the folds are starting to tear and it has new wrinkles. I smooth it out some more.

Anyway, Dave, here's what I want and thanks for asking.

There's a photograph of a window; it takes up most of the page. It's a window that looks into a room. A room inside a home on Christmas Day. There's snow on the window panes, soft and powdery. I can tell it's cold outside because of the frost, but there's moisture on the glass too, so I know it's warm in the room. It's misty and dreamy, and a string of white lights around the window frame invites me to look more closely into the room.

It draws me in.

Inside there's a table set for dinner, Christmas dinner. There are bowls steaming and piled high with potatoes and carrots and peas and stuffing and cranberry sauce. And in the middle of the table, there's the turkey, all brown and glistening, waiting to be carved. A big turkey because, after all, that's what the ad's selling — friggin' turkeys.

Printed at the bottom of the page is "Bring Home a Maple Leaf Turkey, Bring Home a Canadian Tradition." And underneath that, in fancy handwriting like on a Christmas card, it says *Christmas Wishes*.

There are people in the picture, a family. There's a mother at the table ready to carve the turkey. Her two young daughters are sitting side by side, heads close together. And there's a father standing, smiling down at his son, and the son is seated, looking up at his father. I know they're not a real family, but it doesn't matter.

Most of all, there's the glow, the glow that lights up the inside of that room. I know it's just a freakin' turkey ad, but it pulls me in. On some nights it's that glow that keeps me warm.

I fold up my picture and I put it safe, zipped away in my knapsack with my sketchbook. I pick up Dave's beer bottle, figuring I'll finish what's left at the bottom, and I remember my mom laughing. Not the way she laughed today, hungry, thinking about her cigarettes and beer. But the way she used to laugh with me. Full. I put the bottle back down on top of the TV, the beer swishing around inside.

In my room I grab my jean jacket. I pick up the skateboard leaning against the wall, wrapped in Dollarama bags, and I let myself out the door. The elevator smells like piss. I sound like Dave, but piss is piss, and that's what the elevator smells like.

Outside it's snowing, more like freezing rain, hard jabs against my face, pushing my hood back. With the wind sneaking up cold, I stop to button my jacket, tucking the skateboard under my arm so I can put my hands in my pockets. As I turn the corner onto McCaul, the streetlights are just switching on, but they don't spread much light. The CN Tower is a shadow, towering and darkened, behind me.

Near Dundas I stop below the art school, its pick-up-sticks steel legs somehow balancing a whole tabletop building above me. I stop for a moment to watch the students with their portfolios. The Ontario College of Art and Design University, a long name for a dream.

I cross the road, slipping, sliding, working to keep myself from falling, my hands still in my pockets, the skateboard still under my arm.

I don't want to be late.

A neon sign down the street hurries me along. Gleaming pink-red, it says OPEN. As I get closer, I notice most of the *N* is flickering on and off. The sign hangs in a window, a restaurant window, gritty from salt and slush splashed up by snowplows. The electric heater inside has steamed up the glass. There's moisture dripping down, winding trails through the steam, blurring the lights inside.

It's time to go in.

I enter through the alley. The street sounds, the horns, the brakes, the shouts, the sirens fade behind me, hushed and muted. I make my way towards the door. A bare bulb shines enough light for me to avoid the patches of ice and the garbage bins.

I see Dante's back as I open the door. He's flipping burgers and swaying, always singing this one Bruce Springsteen song while he cooks, asking his baby to be in his book of dreams. The sizzling-grease smells rising from the stove remind me I haven't eaten since this morning.

Dante hears me come in and he turns and says, "Mikey, my man."

Only Dante calls me Mikey.

"Mikey, you're just in time." He points towards the sink with his spatula.

I put the skateboard down, and Dante takes my sweatshirt and my jean jacket and he hangs them on a hook beside the mops. He hands me an apron.

I've just started washing the pots when Alison comes into the kitchen. Alison is a waitress. She's beautiful, her long black hair tied back in a ponytail when she's working.

"Did you bring it, Mike?" she asks me.

Dante and Alison watch as I unwrap the plastic bags from around the skateboard. I hand it to Alison, and she looks down at it. In almost a whisper, she says, "It's perfect, Mike. Perfect."

I've painted a portrait of Alison onto the wood. It's a Christmas gift for her boyfriend, Scott, to hang on their bedroom wall. Alison says Scott loves her and skateboards, but he loves Alison more. I painted Alison with her hair down around her shoulders and her eyes looking out at Scott and I made sure when I painted her lips that her smile said, "It's good you love me more than your skateboards, it's really good."

Alison hugs me and she hugs Scott's gift close to her and she carries it into the restaurant. I follow through the swinging door. And Dante goes back to singing his "Book of Dreams."

Alison shows the skateboard to Rosa, Dante's wife,

standing behind the front counter by the cash register. Rosa reaches up, her hands soft on my cheeks. She tells me I have a gift.

She says, "Mike, you'll go to that art school."

I've worked here since October and I'm getting used to Rosa saying things like she knows they're going to happen. Dante says the restaurant is named Rosa's because before they were married, Rosa told Dante he was a good cook. She told him he would own his own restaurant. She told him she would help him.

Sherry gives a table by the window their bill and comes over to the counter to look at the skateboard. Sherry is the other waitress who works at Rosa's. She's older than Alison and she has a little boy, Mac. Sherry's had lots of boyfriends but none of them have loved Mac as much as they've loved Sherry.

"That doesn't mean you give up looking," Sherry tells me.

I wish l could tell Mom that Dave loves his beer more than he loves her. I wish I could tell her not to give up looking, not to give up.

Rosa hands me a new menu. She asks me to copy it out on the chalkboard on the wall across from the counter.

"A job for an artist," she says.

Rosa's words fill me up. I blink my eyes quick to hide my tears.

There aren't many customers tonight so I take my time. I print the words *mashed potatoes* and *vegetables* and *cranberry sauce* and *stuffing*, and *choice of pie, mincemeat or apple à la mode* onto the chalkboard. I have only white chalk but next I draw a turkey, a big turkey, and I highlight and shade it so it looks like it's sitting up there on the chalkboard waiting to be carved. And at the bottom, in fancy handwriting like on a Christmas card, I add, *Christmas Wishes*.

The last of the pots are scrubbed and dried. I sit in a booth, beside the chalkboard.

Rosa's at the table. "Eat," she says, handing me a bowl of soup. From the kitchen I can hear Dante singing something about scars remaining but the pain slipping away, still asking his baby to be in his book of dreams. Alison and Sherry sit across from me, side by side, heads close together. The rhythm of their voices, their laughter, are a chorus for Dante. I think of how I will draw this later in my sketchbook. At home, into my silences, Dave says, "Hey, kid. Cat got your tongue?" But here, in this restaurant with Dante and Rosa and Alison and Sherry, here, my silence is part of their song.

Dante leaves his kitchen and stands by Rosa. He smiles down at me, his hand on my shoulder. He asks, "Mikey, you'll be here? You'll come to Rosa's on Christmas?"

"On Christmas?"

Sherry says, "Dante, where'd you hide it this time?"

She says to me, "I've been telling him for years, frame it and hang it up at the front. Free advertising."

Dante says, "My food is my advertisement."

But he goes behind the counter and comes back with a newspaper article. Cut from the *Toronto Star*, yellowed and faded, edges curling, it says, "Christmas at Rosa's, a Toronto Tradition."

There's a black-and-white photograph of Rosa and Dante wearing their aprons, standing close together with their arms reaching out, opened wide. "Welcome," it looks like they're saying. There are other people crowded into the picture. I recognize Sherry smiling. The article says Rosa and Dante open their restaurant doors on Christmas Day. Every Christmas, for as long as the reporter can remember. It says Rosa and Dante, the two of them, serve dinner to family, friends, employees, customers, anyone who shows up, everyone. The dinner is free, a gift. It says Christmas is the day Rosa and Dante give thanks.

I look up at Dante, the chalkboard framed like a window behind him. And I say, "Yeah, I'll be here."

Rosa's is closed for the night. The lights are dimmed and the neon sign is turned off. But it's not dark. There's a glow.

## Acknowledgments

On my desk there is a collection of sticky notes. Sticky notes of written names. Names of people I want to thank. Thank for helping me with this book. This book that wouldn't be possible without you, each and every one of you.

First sticky note: Dr. Alan Ing. First, because, if not for you, I wouldn't be here writing names on sticky notes. We met serendipitously, but it isn't serendipity that I owe my life to. Thank you, Alan.

Second sticky note: Winnie Croza. Fifteen years ago, you sent me a note. It said, "I always thought that someday you would write a book." I'd never told you my dream of becoming a writer. Somehow, you knew. I wish you were here to see this book. Somehow, I think you are. Thank you, Winnie.

Third sticky note: Kathie Wilson and Mike Wilson. Once upon a time, you enthusiastically hosted a book launch for the prototype of this book. Regarding any present-day launches, kindly contact my agent, M.W., for a rider listing my preferences. Thank you, Kathie and Mike.

Fourth sticky note: Peter Carver and Tim Wynne-Jones. You read (at one stage or another) some of the stories in this book and offered invaluable suggestions. Thank you, Peter and Tim.

Fifth sticky note: Beth Kaplan. Teacher/mentor/friend. You read every story (at one stage or another) in this book and offered invaluable encouragement. Thank you, Beth.

Sixth sticky note: Wendy Mason. You are a passionate and tireless promoter of Canadian children's literature. Thank you, Wendy.

Seventh sticky note: Bernie Goedhart. When we (finally) met in person, you asked me what I was working on. I said I'd been writing a story about a doll but I'd stopped because I thought it was too weird. You said, "Weird is good." Thank you, Bernie.

Eighth sticky note: Kelsey Garrity-Riley. You created a swirly and dreamy, beautiful cover (I want to paint a room in my home that exact same orange) and interior art. Thank you, Kelsey.

Ninth sticky note: Groundwood Books. You are special and unique, and I am so very proud to be published by you. Thank you, Groundwood.

Tenth sticky note: Groundwood team. Groundwood Books is what it is because of you. Your reflection. Thank you, Michael, Nan, Shelley, Fred, Cindy and, especially (for your thoughtful edit and your patience with my 9:00 a.m. emails), Emma.

Eleventh sticky note: Sheila Barry. Publisher/editor/human extraordinaire. Anyone who has met you knows I am not exaggerating. Thank you, Sheila.

Twelfth sticky note: My family. You are my best critics because you love everything I write and you are my worst critics because you love everything I write. For this (and a few other reasons) I love you. Thank you, Mike, Shannon, Caitie, Allie, Jake, Aidan, Andrew, Terence, Lorraine, Keaton, Porter, Archie and Hunter. xoxo

Final note: Sheila Barry, 1963–2017. There wasn't supposed to be a final note. You were supposed to stay where I put you, securely stuck, in between your Groundwood team and my family. You weren't supposed to become unstuck. But you did. And so — with love and tears and profound sadness — I remember.

The first time I met you for coffee we ended up talking about (no surprise) picture books, their magic, their power, the ones we loved the most. How they were often dismissed (mostly by adult book lovers) for being too simple. You mentioned a book — I believe you said it was one of your favorites — *Duck, Death and the Tulip*. You said that with a few simple words and illustrations, it spoke of death (and, therefore, also life) like no adult book ever could. You said it was the book you used to convert the doubters and that, in fact, the next day, you were meeting with a colleague (an adult book editor who wasn't fond of children's books) to give her a copy.

Of course, the moment I got home, I ordered the book.

And the moment it arrived, I read it.

I emailed you, "NOT simple. Duck's eyes, wow, those eyes. Beautiful. I cried."

You replied, "It still makes me cry every time I read it."

I cry as I reread the book.

I cry as I write this.

I thought there would be many more coffees, many more talks about books.

I hope you knew how much you meant to me. I think you did. Sheila, with all my heart, thank you.